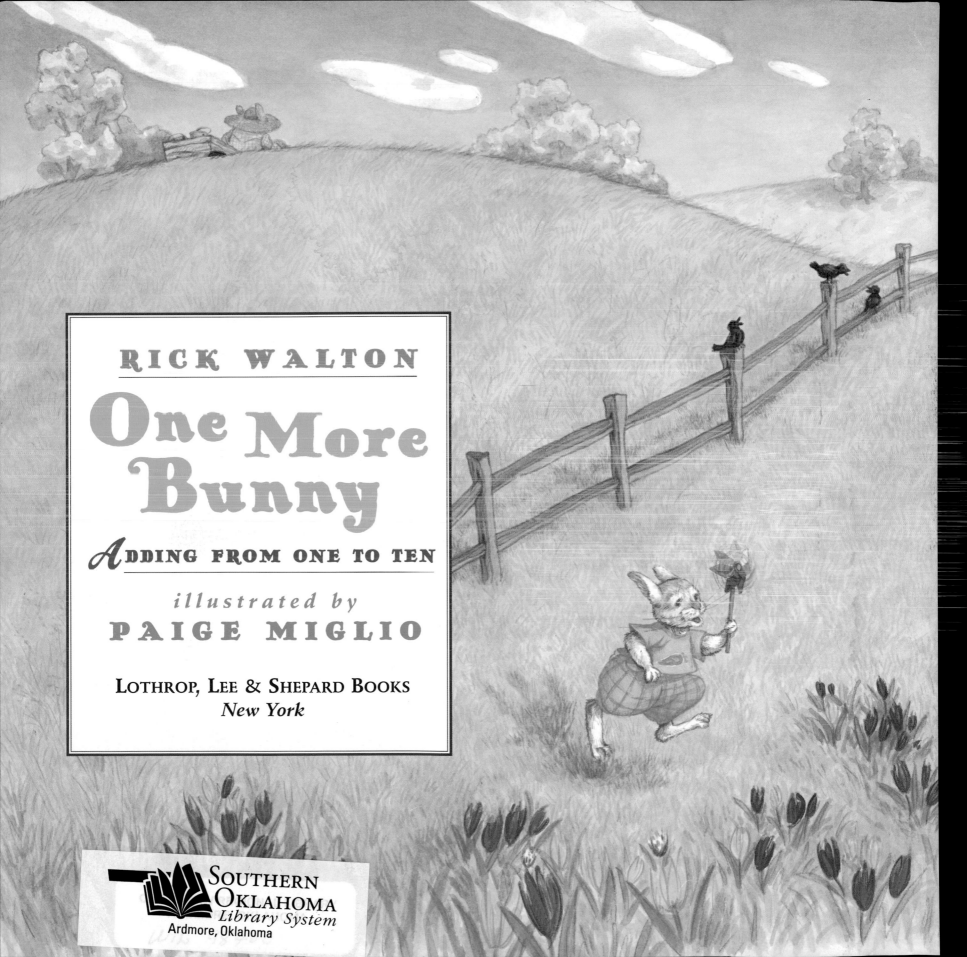

RICK WALTON

One More Bunny

Adding from One to Ten

illustrated by
PAIGE MIGLIO

LOTHROP, LEE & SHEPARD BOOKS
New York

To Bill and Wendy Walton, and their bunnies
Tylor, Alisha, Zachary, and Christian
—RW

For my Grammy and Pop-Pop, and in loving memory of
Tinker and Grammy-Daddy
—PM

Colored pencils on watercolor were used for
the full-color illustrations.
The text type is Schneidler 22-point.

Text copyright © 2000 by Rick Walton
Illustrations copyright © 2000 by Paige Miglio
Published by Lothrop, Lee & Shepard Books
a division of William Morrow and Company, Inc.
1350 Avenue of the Americas, New York, NY 10019
www.williammorrow.com

Printed in Hong Kong by South China
Printing Company (1988) Ltd.

LIBRARY OF CONGRESS CATALOGING-IN-PUBLICATION DATA
Walton, Rick. One more bunny: adding from one to ten/by Rick Walton;
illustrations by Paige Miglio   p. cm.
Summary: Bunnies frolicking at the playground introduce the
numbers one through ten and the principles of simple addition.
ISBN 0-688-16847-7 (trade)   ISBN 0-688-16848-5 (library)
[1. Counting. 2. Rabbits—Fiction. 3. Stories in rhyme.]
I. Miglio, Paige, ill. II. Title.
PZ8.3.W199Om 2000   [E]—dc21 99-27642 CIP
1 3 5 7 9 10 8 6 4 2

1 = 1

1 little bunny
Sitting on the slide.
Let's go, bunny.
What a ride!

Here comes one more bunny.

$$\text{🐰} + \text{🐰} = 2$$

$$\begin{array}{r} 1 \\ + 1 \\ \hline 2 \end{array}$$

2 little bunnies
Tossing a ball.
Catch, bunnies, catch.
Don't let it fall.

Here comes one more bunny.

$$\text{🐰} + \text{🐰} + \text{🐰} = 3$$

$$\begin{array}{r} 2 \\ + 1 \\ \hline 3 \end{array}$$

3 little bunnies
Swing to the sky.
Up, bunnies, up.
Flying high!

Here comes one more bunny.

$$\text{🐰} + \text{🐰} + \text{🐰} + \text{🐰} = 4$$

$$\begin{array}{cc} 2 & 3 \\ +\,2 & +\,1 \\ \hline 4 & 4 \end{array}$$

4 little bunnies,
Feet off the ground.
Bunnies get dizzy on the
Merry-go-round.

Here comes one more bunny.

$$\text{🐰} + \text{🐰} + \text{🐰} + \text{🐰} + \text{🐰} = 5$$

$$
\begin{array}{cc}
3 & 4 \\
+\ 2 & +\ 1 \\
\hline
5 & 5
\end{array}
$$

5 little bunnies,
Jump ropes spin.
Skip, bunnies, skip.
My turn in!

Here comes one more bunny.

$$\text{🐰} + \text{🐰} + \text{🐰} + \text{🐰} + \text{🐰} + \text{🐰} = 6$$

$$
\begin{array}{ccc}
3 & 4 & 5 \\
+3 & +2 & +1 \\
\hline
6 & 6 & 6
\end{array}
$$

6 little bunnies,
Lickety-split.
Run, bunnies, run.
Tag, you're it!

Here comes one more bunny.

$$\text{🐰} + \text{🐰} + \text{🐰} + \text{🐰} + \text{🐰} + \text{🐰} + \text{🐰} = 7$$

$$\begin{array}{r} 4 \\ + 3 \\ \hline 7 \end{array} \qquad \begin{array}{r} 5 \\ + 2 \\ \hline 7 \end{array} \qquad \begin{array}{r} 6 \\ + 1 \\ \hline 7 \end{array}$$

7 little bunnies.
Every bunny dig.
Scoop, bunnies, scoop.
That hole's big!

Here comes one more bunny.

$$🐰 + 🐰 + 🐰 + 🐰 +$$
$$🐰 + 🐰 + 🐰 + 🐰 = 8$$

$$\begin{array}{r} 4 \\ + 4 \\ \hline 8 \end{array} \qquad \begin{array}{r} 5 \\ + 3 \\ \hline 8 \end{array} \qquad \begin{array}{r} 6 \\ + 2 \\ \hline 8 \end{array} \qquad \begin{array}{r} 7 \\ + 1 \\ \hline 8 \end{array}$$

8 little bunnies.
Up they go.
Jungle gym bunnies,
High and low.

Here comes one more bunny.

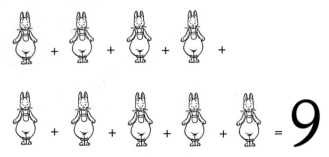 = **9**

$$\begin{array}{r} 5 \\ + 4 \\ \hline 9 \end{array} \qquad \begin{array}{r} 6 \\ + 3 \\ \hline 9 \end{array} \qquad \begin{array}{r} 7 \\ + 2 \\ \hline 9 \end{array} \qquad \begin{array}{r} 8 \\ + 1 \\ \hline 9 \end{array}$$

9 little bunnies
Hide and seek.
Stay still, bunnies.
Shhh—don't speak!

Here comes one more bunny.

$$\text{🐰} + \text{🐰} + \text{🐰} + \text{🐰} + \text{🐰} + \text{🐰} + \text{🐰} + \text{🐰} + \text{🐰} + \text{🐰} = 10$$

$$
\begin{array}{ccccc}
5 & 6 & 7 & 8 & 9 \\
+\,5 & +\,4 & +\,3 & +\,2 & +\,1 \\
\hline
10 & 10 & 10 & 10 & 10
\end{array}
$$

10 happy bunnies.

"Hi, Mom, hi!"

"Time to go home now."

'Bye, bunnies, 'bye.

There are many things besides bunnies to count and add in this book:

One bunny 1 pinwheel

Two bunnies $1 + 1 = 2$ butterflies

Three bunnies $2 + 1 = 3$ leaves

Four bunnies $3 + 1 = 4$ blackberries $2 + 2 = 4$ bees

Five bunnies $4 + 1 = 5$ trees $3 + 2 = 5$ raspberries

Six bunnies $5 + 1 = 6$ yellow flowers in the necklace $4 + 2 = 6$ ladybugs $3 + 3 = 6$ rocks

---

Seven bunnies 6 orange $+ 1$ blue $= 7$ shovels $5 + 2 = 7$ crocuses   4 blue $+ 3$ yellow $= 7$ stripes on the bucket

---

Eight bunnies $7 + 1 = 8$ morning glories $6 + 2 = 8$ inchworms $5 + 3 = 8$ knotholes $4 + 4 = 8$ robin's eggs

---

Nine bunnies $8 + 1 = 9$ dragonflies $7 + 2 = 9$ mushrooms $6 + 3 = 9$ blackbirds $5 + 4 = 9$ railing posts

---

Ten bunnies $9 + 1 = 10$ yellow tulips $8 + 2 = 10$ ants $7 + 3 = 10$ strawberries $6 + 4 = 10$ carrots
5 blue $+ 5$ pink $= 10$ flowers on Mom's skirt